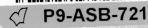

To the victims of the Black Forest fire and of wildfires everywhere. To the brave people who risk their lives to fight the fires. To the scientists developing solutions to slow down the effects of climate change. And to all those, young and old, who keep pushing for the changes that will save our planet. –AC

For Michael –DP

Hello, Tree

Written by
Ana Crespo

Illustrated by
Dow Phumiruk

L B

Little, Brown and Company
New York Boston

I met the girl when
she was a baby…

and I was just a sapling.

I helped her with
her first steps.

We played together.

"Hello, Tree!"

She dressed me up.

And we spent countless nights wishing upon the stars.

But the girl wasn't my only friend.

I had never felt alone, until that hot and
windy summer night.

It was a swallow who called it first.

"Fire's coming!"

And the animals ran away.

Even the insects tried to flee.

The girl and her family left, too.

All I could do…was wait.

Wait as roaring flames breathed smoke into the sky.

And left only a single star to wish upon.

It must have been
my lucky one.

Rescue came…

on the ground…

and in the skies.

Many gray days and orange nights passed.

Until fire lost the battle.

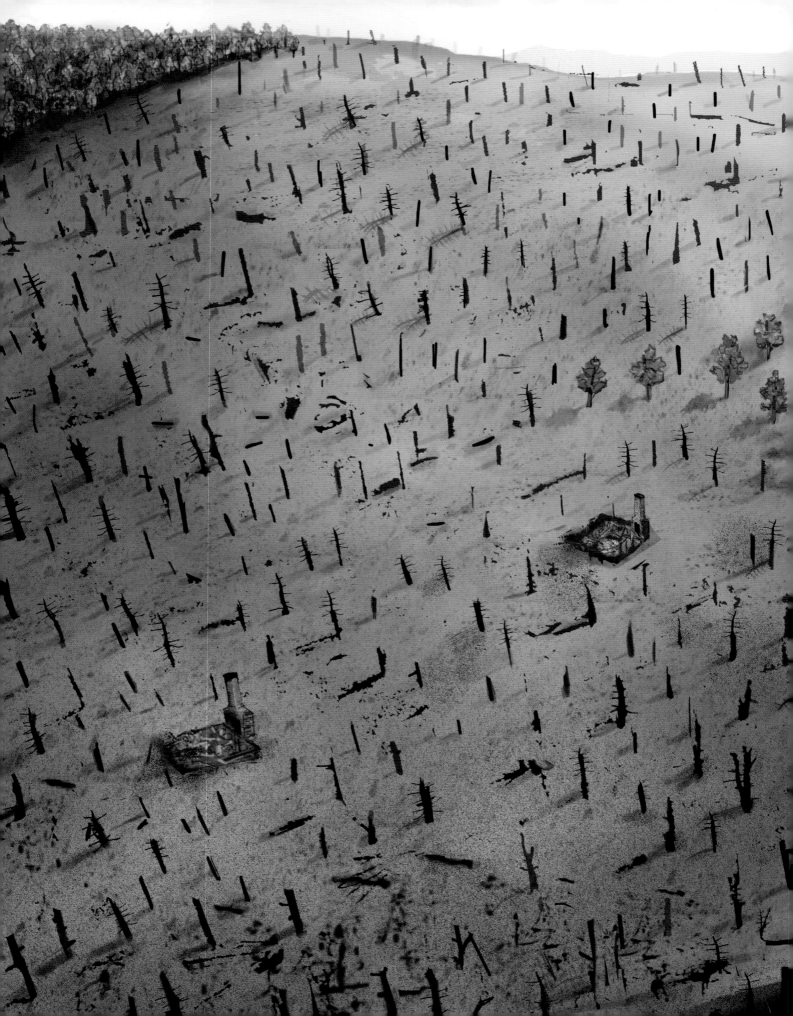

And the forest was still.

But it wasn't still for too long.

Workers came.

And left.

Only then was the girl allowed to visit.

"Hello, Tree!"

I was so happy to see her again.

Fall flew by.

Winter tried to stay.

At last, spring arrived.

New flowers sprouted all around.

And a bluebird family moved nearby.

The forest had changed.

When volunteers brought in seedlings, we all wished for them to grow fast.

But they didn't.

The seedlings grew slowly.

Slower than the girl.

Soon, she was ready to see other skies.
To wish upon new stars.

Like the bluebirds, she left, too.

But the girl wasn't my only friend.

And I never felt alone again.

"Hello, Tree. I missed you!"

FIRE BEGINS

Many wildfires start with lightning or another natural occurrence, but most of them are sparked by humans.

Even a tiny leftover ember from a campfire can start a wildfire.

Low-hanging branches and undergrowth serve as fuel for the fire.

Some plants have defense mechanisms to protect them from fires.

The thick bark of a ponderosa pine tree makes it fire-resistant.

During a fire, most animals run away or hide, but some take advantage of the situation.

A swallow munches on fleeing insects.

A raccoon awaits to snack on a rodent.

FIREFIGHTERS TO THE RESCUE

Fire has always played an important role in the life cycle of forests.

Usually, only wildfires that threaten human lives or properties are fought.

Aircraft aid the fight by dropping water and fire retardant.

Often, ground crews create a fuel-free line to prevent the fire from spreading.

Global warming affects the intensity of wildfires and makes them harder to fight.

It may take over a month to fully extinguish a wildfire.

SHORTLY AFTER THE FIRE

Some animals thrive in recently burned forests.

Some beetles come to the burning forest to mate and lay their eggs.

A hairy woodpecker comes to eat the beetles.

Extreme heat opens a lodgepole pinecone buried under the soil, releasing its seeds.

Although charred, some ponderosa pine trees survive the fire because their insides are preserved.

The lack of vegetation on burned scars makes it harder for the soil to absorb water, leaving the area prone to erosion.

Crews remove debris and place protective structures to slow down erosion and prevent flooding and mudslides.

THE FIRST SPRING AND THE BENEFITS OF FIRE

Sunlight reaches the ground and helps the lodgepole pine seeds turn into seedlings.

The sun also helps germinate wildflower seeds that had been dormant underground.

Bees come after the nectar the wildflowers provide.

A bluebird makes a nest in a woodpecker's hole on a tree snag.

The clearing of the understory allows a new aspen tree to sprout.

Ponderosa pine seedlings grow, thanks to the wind and animals who brought the seeds to the burned area.

Volunteers plant new seedlings that will also help combat erosion.

SOME SPRINGS LATER

The wildflowers help restore the nutrients in the soil.

The nutrients help the understory grow.

The small aspen tree is now an aspen grove.

MANY SPRINGS LATER

Pine trees grow higher.

There's less sunlight reaching the understory.

Wildflowers don't bloom as much.

Aspen groves are not as common anymore.

There are more deer around.

And the forest starts to look more like it did before the fire.

About This Book

The illustrations for this book were created with Photoshop and include scanned watercolor and pencil textures. This book was edited by Alvina Ling and designed by Sasha Illingworth and Angelie Yap. The production was supervised by Lillian Sun, and the production editor was Annie McDonnell. The text was set in Adobe Caslon Pro, and the display type is hand lettered.

References

Boehle, Tina and Daniel Buckley (National Park Services Division of Wildfire and Aviation Management), interview by Ana Crespo, unpublished, conducted by e-mail on February 16, 2017.

National Park Service. "Post Wildland Fire Programs." Last updated November 15, 2018. https://www.nps.gov/subjects/fire/post-wildland-fire-programs.htm

National Park Service. "Series: Wildland Fire–Learning in Depth." Accessed on August 11, 2020. https://www.nps.gov/articles/series.htm?id=ED398874-1DD8-B71B-0B594AA554EB0E8C

National Park Service. "Wildfire Causes and Evaluations" Last updated November 27, 2018. https://www.nps.gov/articles/wildfire-causes-and-evaluation.htm

Nuccitelli, Dana. "The Many Ways Climate Change Worsens California Wildfires." Yale Climate Connection, November 13, 2018. https://yaleclimateconnections.org/2018/11/the-many-ways-climate-change-worsens-california-wildfires/

Zielinski, Sarah. "What Do Wild Animals Do in a Wildfire?" *National Geographic*, July 22, 2014. https://www.nationalgeographic.com/news/2014/7/140721-animals-wildlife-wildfires-nation-forests-science/

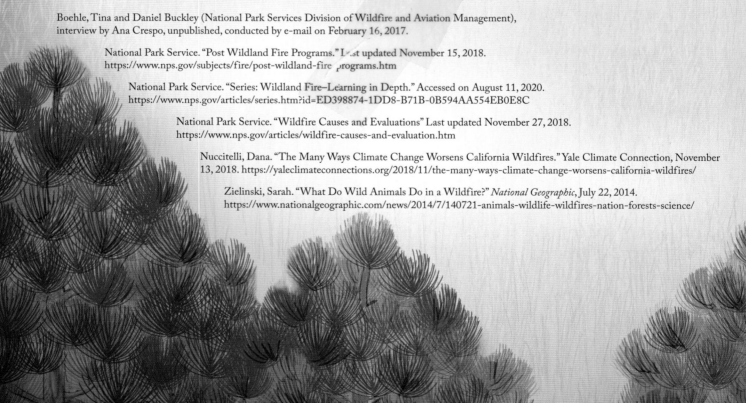